Sports Illustrated KIDS

GRAPHIC NOVELS

STONE ARCH BOOKS
a capstone imprint

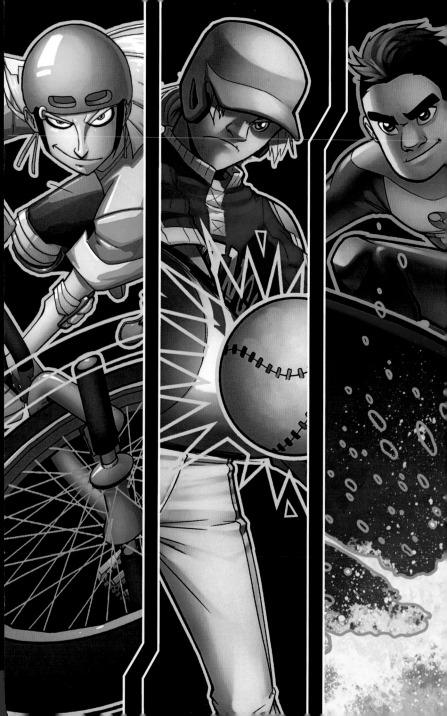

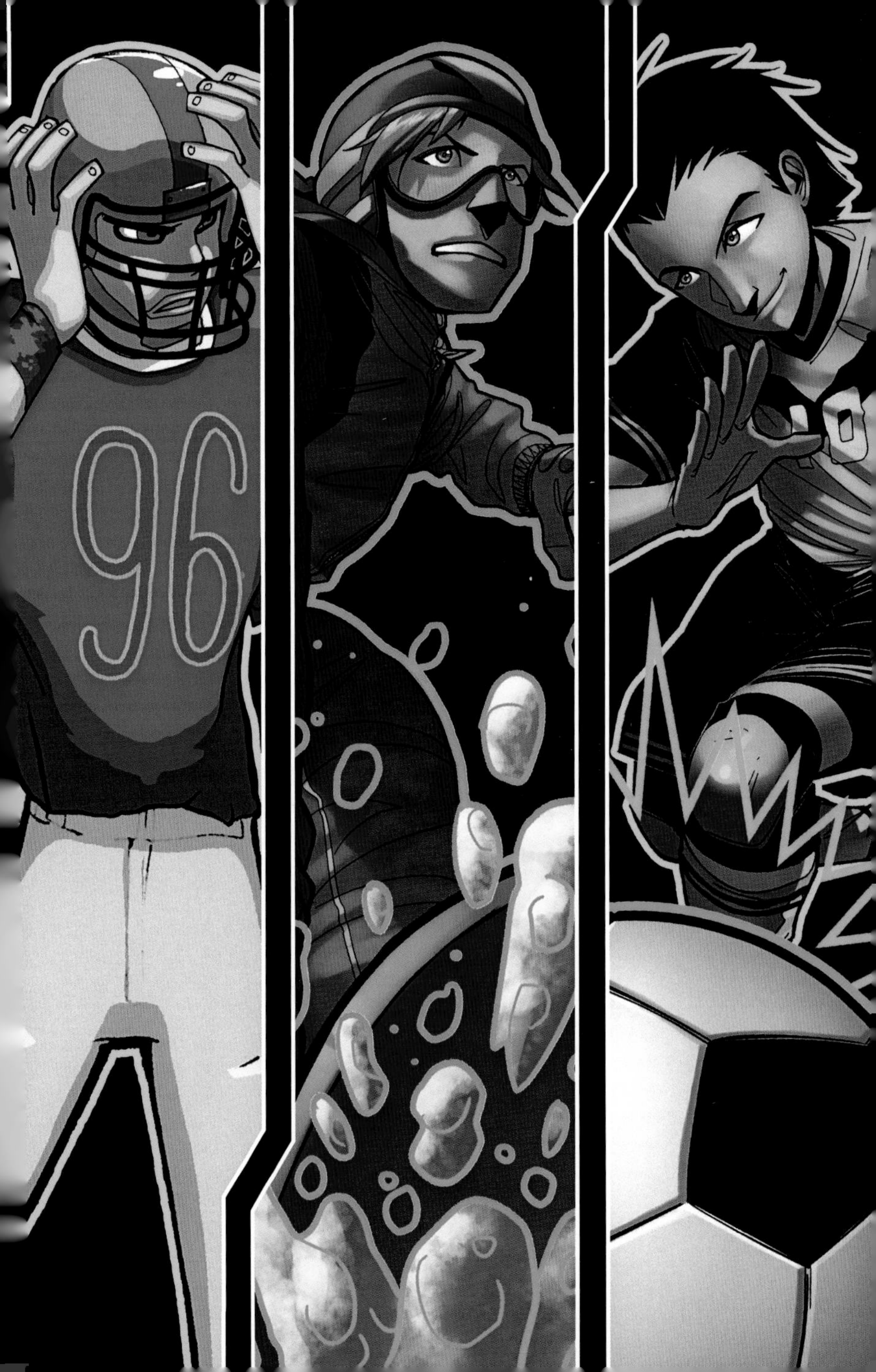

UP NEXT ›››

on Sports Illustrated KIDS

:02 SPORTS ZONE SPECIAL REPORT

:04 FEATURE PRESENTATION:

RIPTIDE PRIDE

FOLLOWED BY:

:50 SPORTS ZONE POSTGAME RECAP

:51 SPORTS ZONE POSTGAME EXTRA

:52 SI KIDS INFO CENTER

BREAKER BAY DECLARED OFF-LIMITS TO SURFERS DUE TO HIG

SIK TICKER

SPORTS ZONE
SPECIAL REPORT

SRF SURFING
PNT PAINTBALL
SNO SNOWBOARDING
SKT SKATEBOARDING
BMX BMX RACING

TEENS TO BRAVE BREAKER BAY'S DEADLY WAVES

TANE KALANA

STATS:
AGE: 14

BIO: Like many athletes, Tane is very superstitious. He believes his surfboard, Lucy, is the only reason he's any good at surfing. However, Tane is as laid back and relaxed as they get. He'd rather surf some waves and relax on the beach than pretty much anything else. But when Cody Hannigan challenges Tane to a surf-off on Breaker Bay, Tane balks. The jagged rocks and strong undertow are dangerous even on the luckiest day.

Sports Illustrated KIDS

UP NEXT: RIPTIDE PRIDE

CODY BRANNIGAN

AGE: 14

BIO: Everyone knows that Cody is a talented surfer, but no one's sure when he's telling the truth about his surfing stories. He has been known to exaggerate, and can also be a bit of a bully at times.

BLZ vs BHS
3-1

TGR vs RDR
33-32

EAG vs BAN
14-7

SPA vs WLD
4-3

BAN vs RDR
21-15

RDR vs LIG
4-3

BLZ vs BHS
3-1

LIA SAGE

AGE: 14

BIO: Tane's best friend and surfing buddy, Lia, is confident and relaxed on — and off — the waves.

OLIVER THOMAS

AGE: 14

BIO: Ollie is one of Cody's buddies. He tends to go with the flow and almost always agrees with anything Cody says.

LUCY

BRAND: CRESCENT FRESH SURFING, INC.

BIO: Lucy is Tane's lucky surfboard. Originally, the board belonged to Summer Kalana, Tane's mother, a former surfing champ.

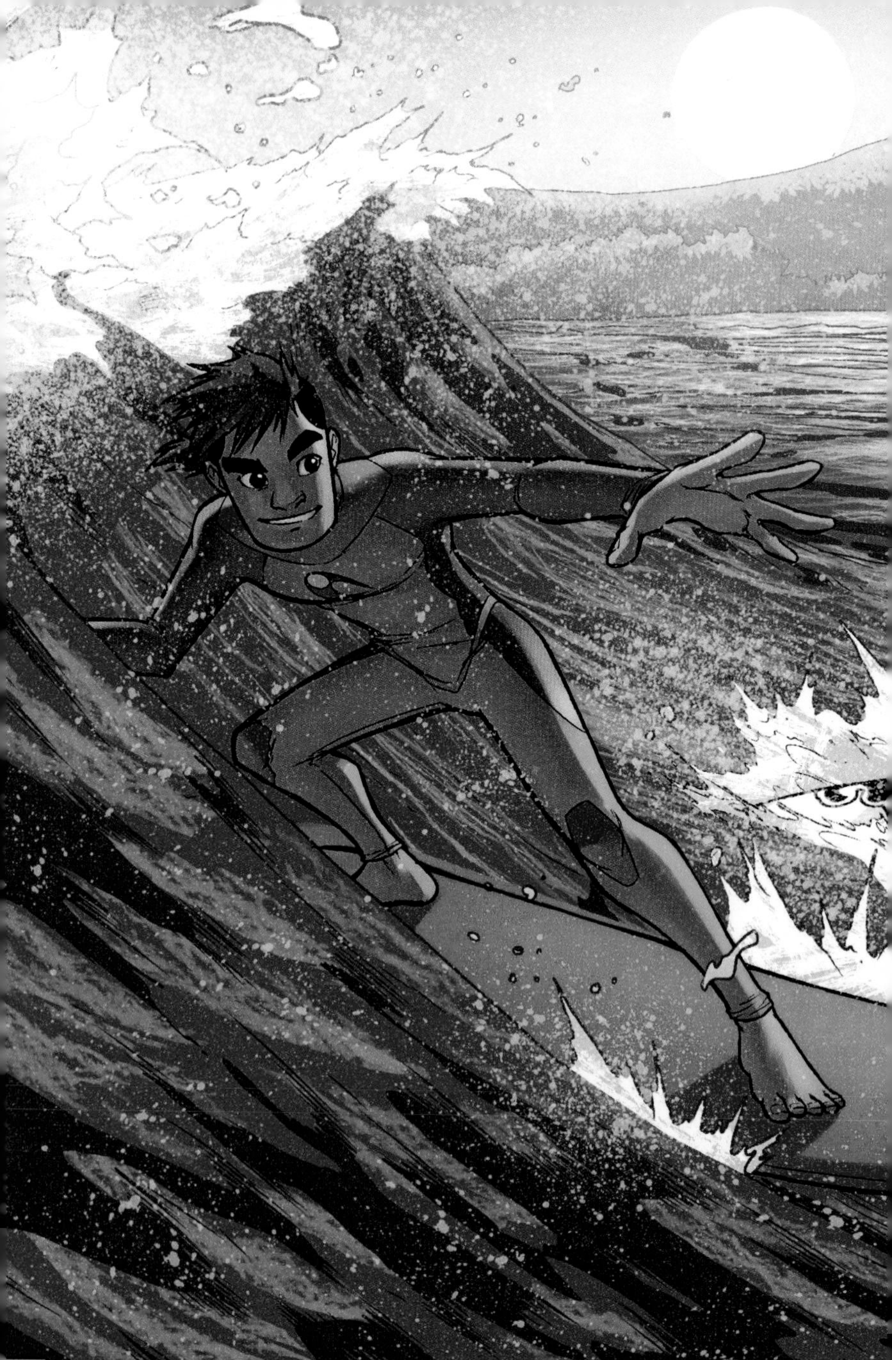

ODAY'S WEATHER REPORT: CLEAR SKIES, A HIGH TEMPERATURE OF 97, A

Sports Illustrated KIDS

PRESENTS

RIPTIDE PRIDE

A PRODUCTION OF

STONE ARCH BOOKS
a capstone imprint

written by Brandon Terrell
penciled by Fernando Cano
inked by Andres Esparza
colored by Fernando Cano

designed and directed by Bob Lentz
edited by Sean Tulien
creative direction by Heather Kinds
editorial management by Donald Le
editorial direction by Michael Dahl

Sports Illustrated KIDS *Riptide Pride* is published by Stone Arch Books,
1710 Roe Crest Drive, North Mankato, Minnesota 56003.
www.capstonepub.com

Summary: Tane Kalana rides waves with ease and looks good doing it. But being talented tends to put a target on your back, and Cody Hannigan has his sights set on taking Tane down a notch. Cody challenges him to a surfer showdown — at Breaker Bay! The infamous surfing locale is known to be unpredictable and dangerous, but Tane is tired of Cody's bullying.

Library of Congress Cataloging-in-Publication Data
Terrell, Brandon, 1978-
Riptide pride / written by Brandon Terrell ; illustrated by Fernand
Andres Esparza
p. cm. -- (Sports illustrated kids graphic novels)
ISBN 978-1-4342-2238-1 (library binding)
ISBN 978-1-4342-3399-8 (paperback)
ISBN 978-1-4342-4954-8 (e-book)
1. Surfing--Comic books, strips, etc. 2. Surfing--Juvenile fiction. 3. and vanity--Comic books, strips, etc. [1. Graphic novels. 2. Surfing-- 3. Pride and vanity--Fiction. 4. Hawaii--Fiction.] I. Cano, Fernando, il Esparza, Andres, ill. IV. Title. V. Series: Sports illustrated kids graph novels.
PZ7.7.T46Ri 2012
741.5'973--dc22 2011008308

Printed in the United States of America.
002868

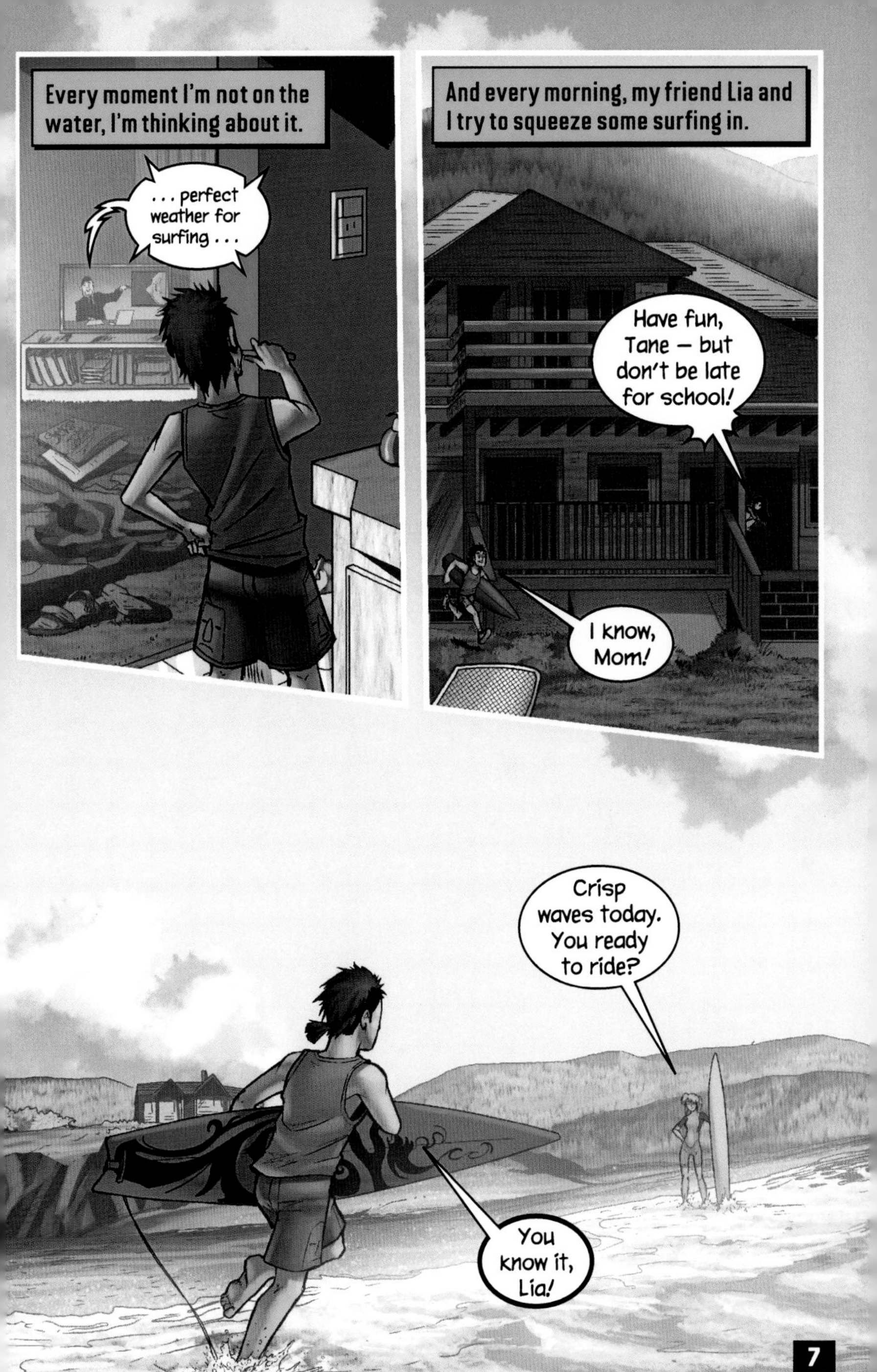

Every moment I'm not on the water, I'm thinking about it.
. . . perfect weather for surfing . . .
And every morning, my friend Lia and I try to squeeze some surfing in.
Have fun, Tane — but don't be late for school!
I know, Mom!
Crisp waves today. You ready to ride?
You know it, Lia!

My name is Tane Kalana.
People say I'm one of the best surfers around.
My response to that?
WOOO-HOOO

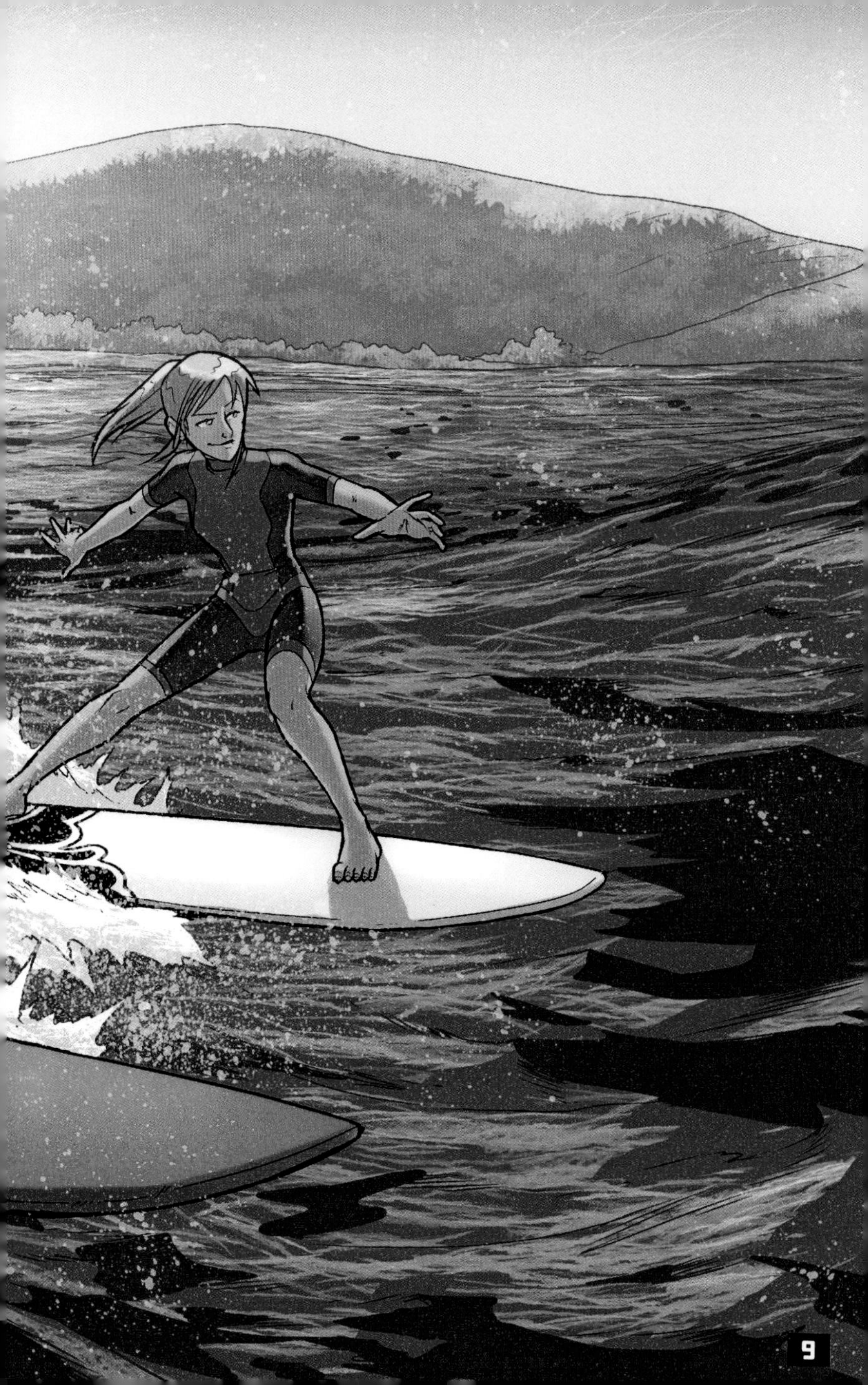

Like a lot of athletes, I'm also really superstitious.

I believe most of my surfing skills come from my surfboard, Lucy.

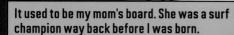

It used to be my mom's board. She was a surf champion way back before I was born.

But now it's all mine.

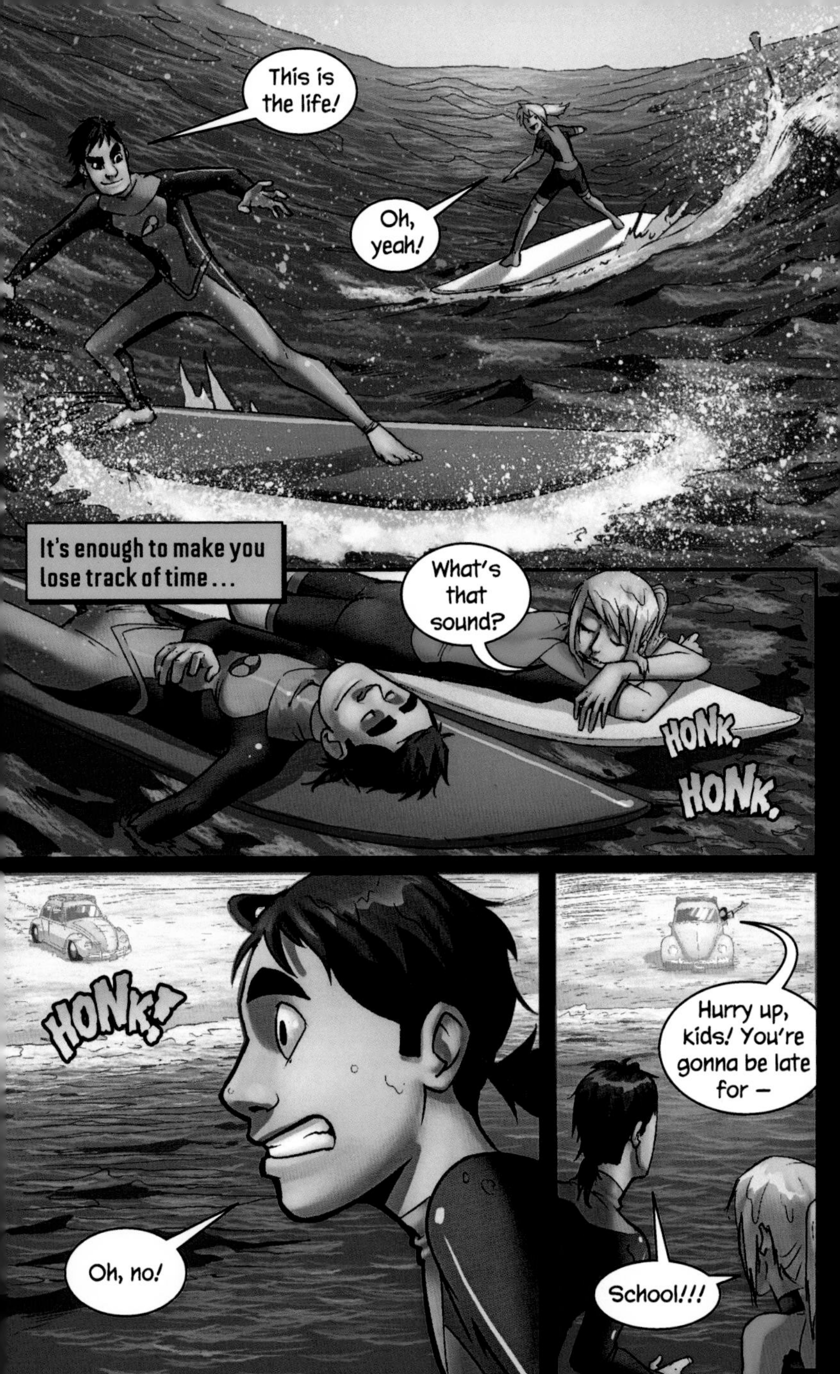
This is the life!
Oh, yeah!
It's enough to make you lose track of time . . .
What's that sound?
HONK.
HONK.
HONK!
Hurry up, kids! You're gonna be late for –
Oh, no!
School!!!

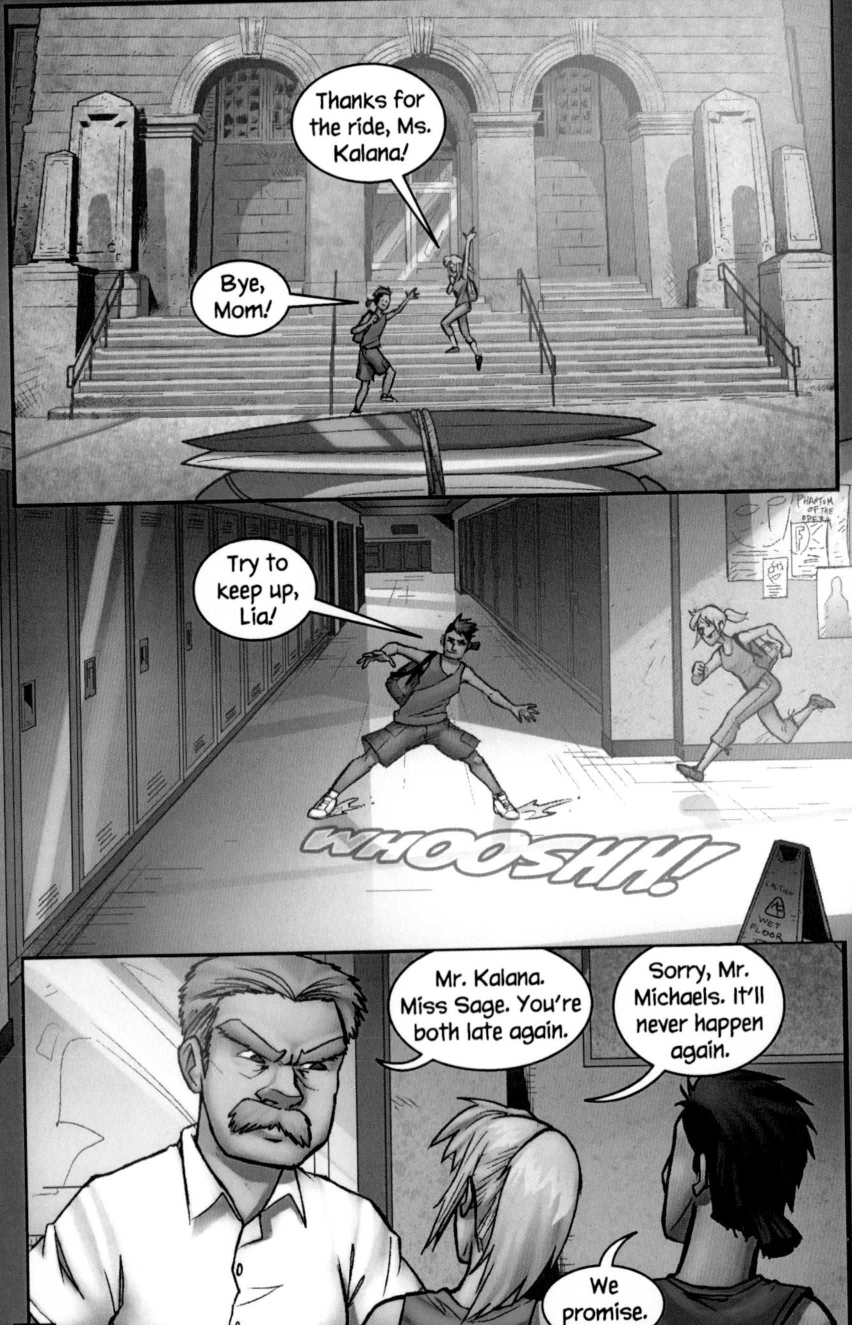
Thanks for the ride, Ms. Kalana!
Bye, Mom!
Try to keep up, Lia!
WHOOSHH!
PHANTOM OF THE OPERA
CAUTION WET FLOOR
Mr. Kalana. Miss Sage. You're both late again.
Sorry, Mr. Michaels. It'll never happen again.
We promise.

19

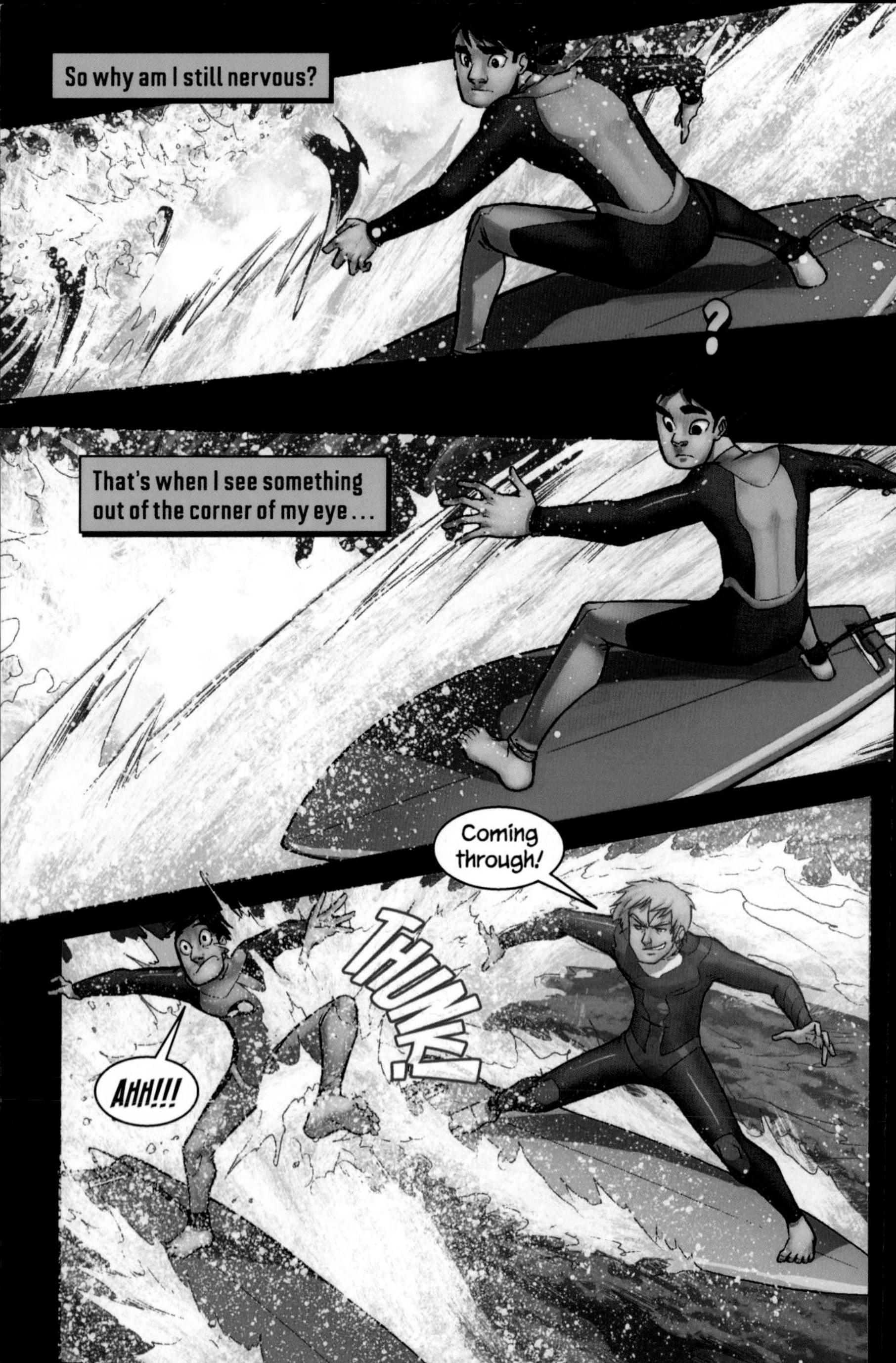
So why am I still nervous?
?
That's when I see something out of the corner of my eye . . .
Coming through!
THUNK!
AHH!!!

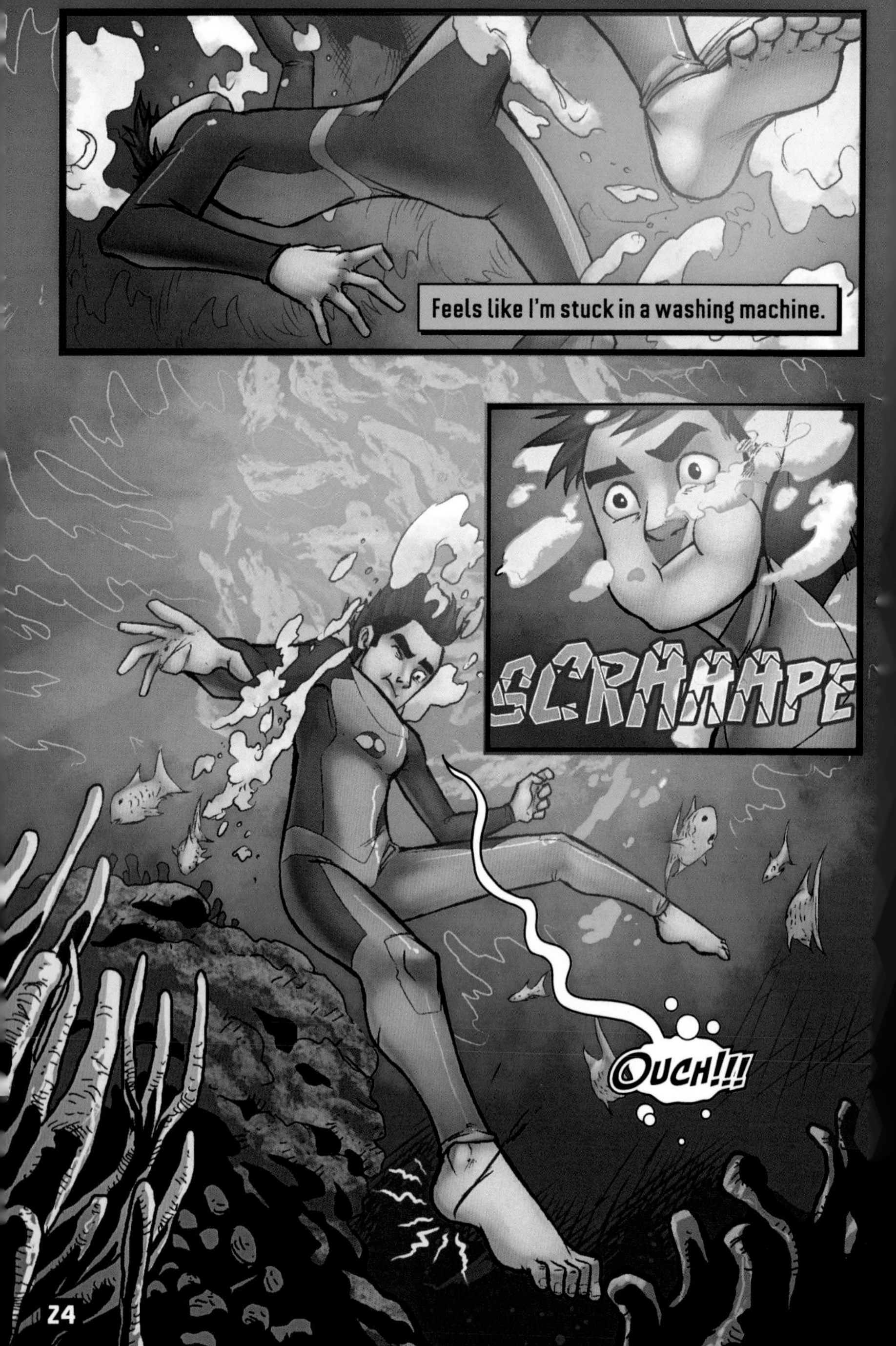
Feels like I'm stuck in a washing machine.
SCRAAAAPE
OUCH!!!

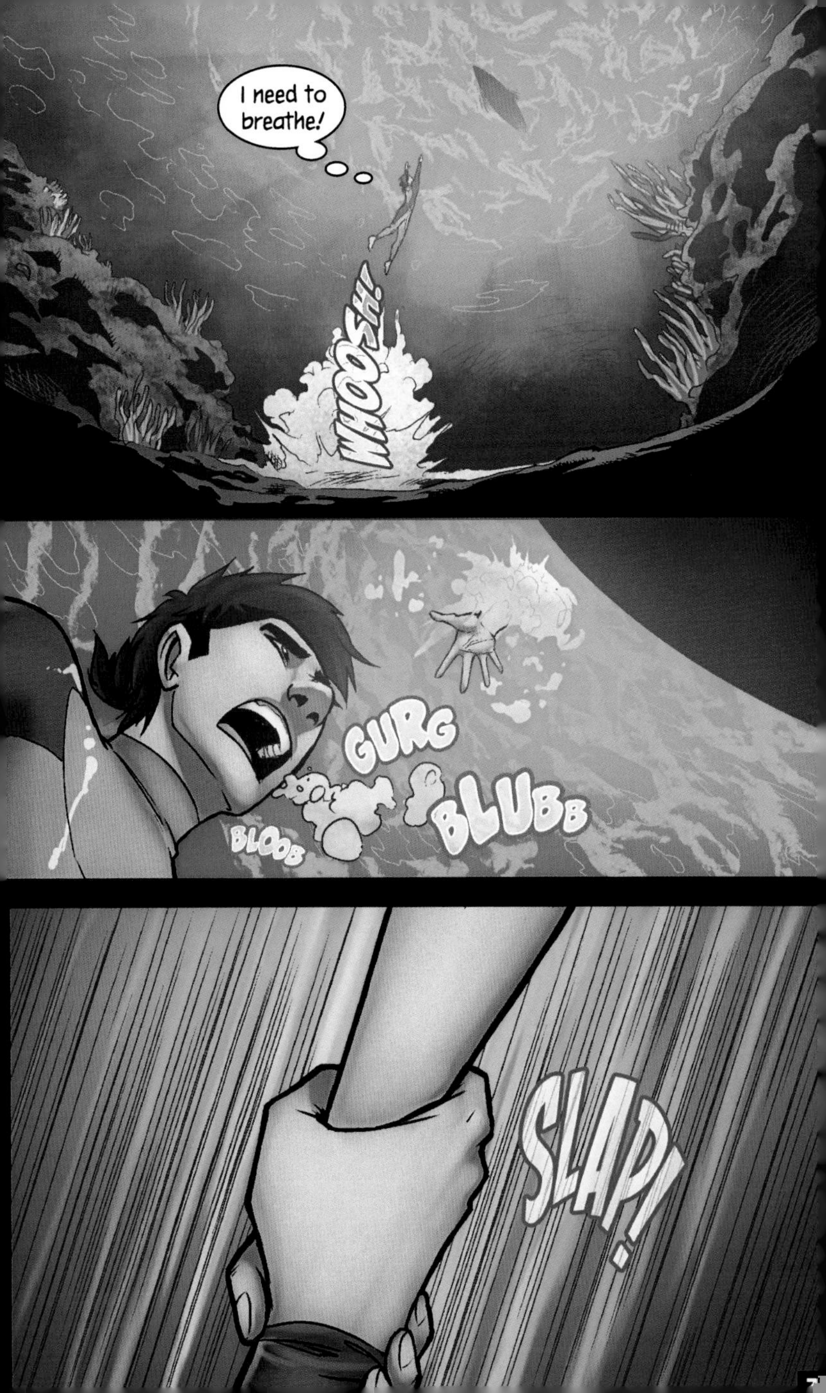
I need to breathe!
WHOOSH!
GURG
BLUBB
BLOOB
SLAP!

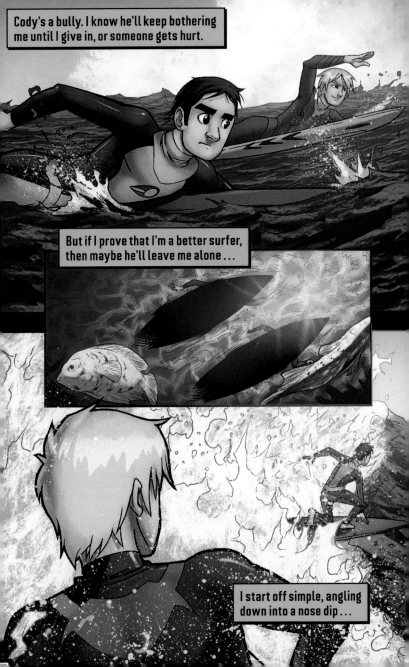

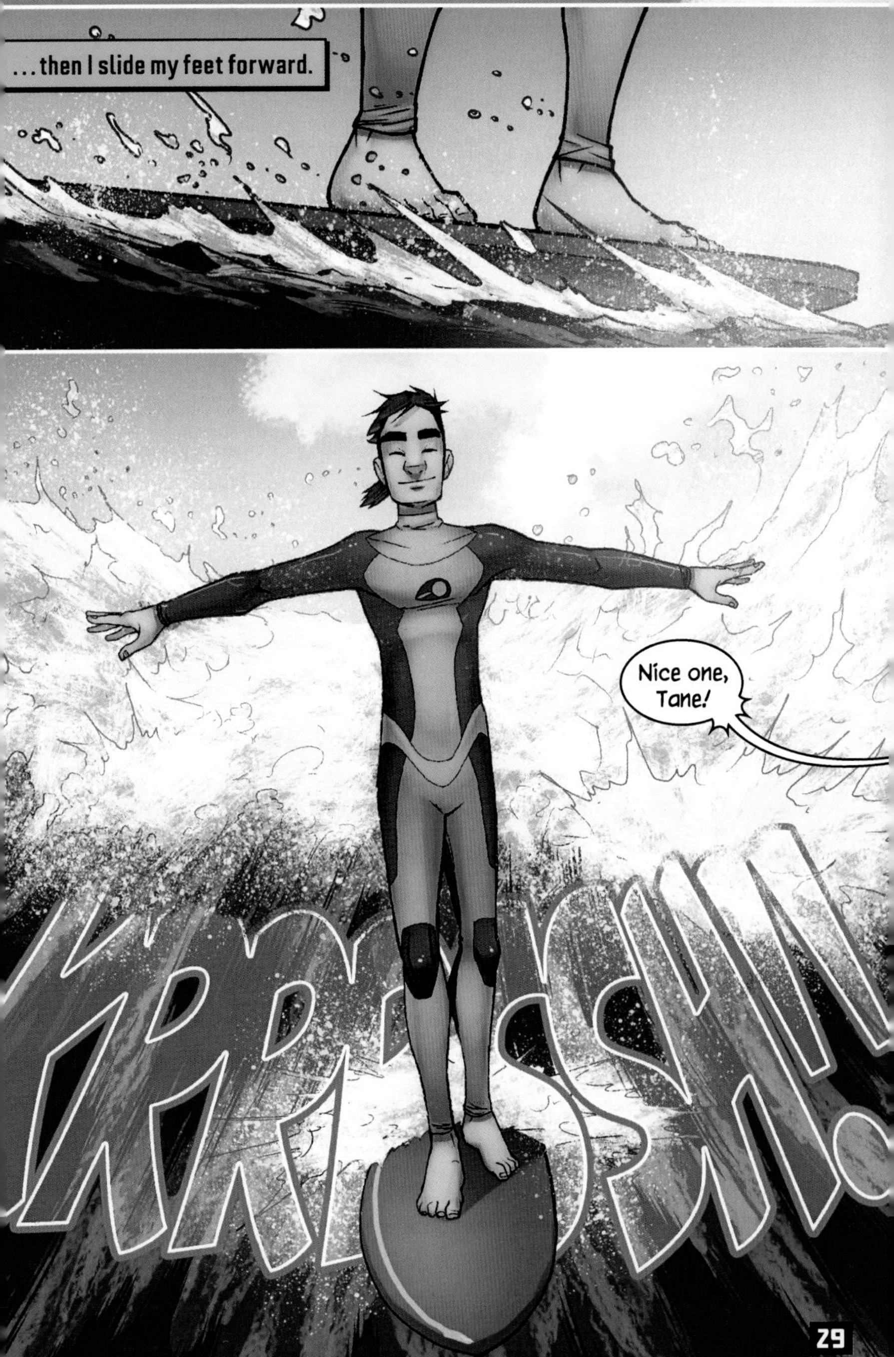
...then I slide my feet forward.
Nice one, Tane!

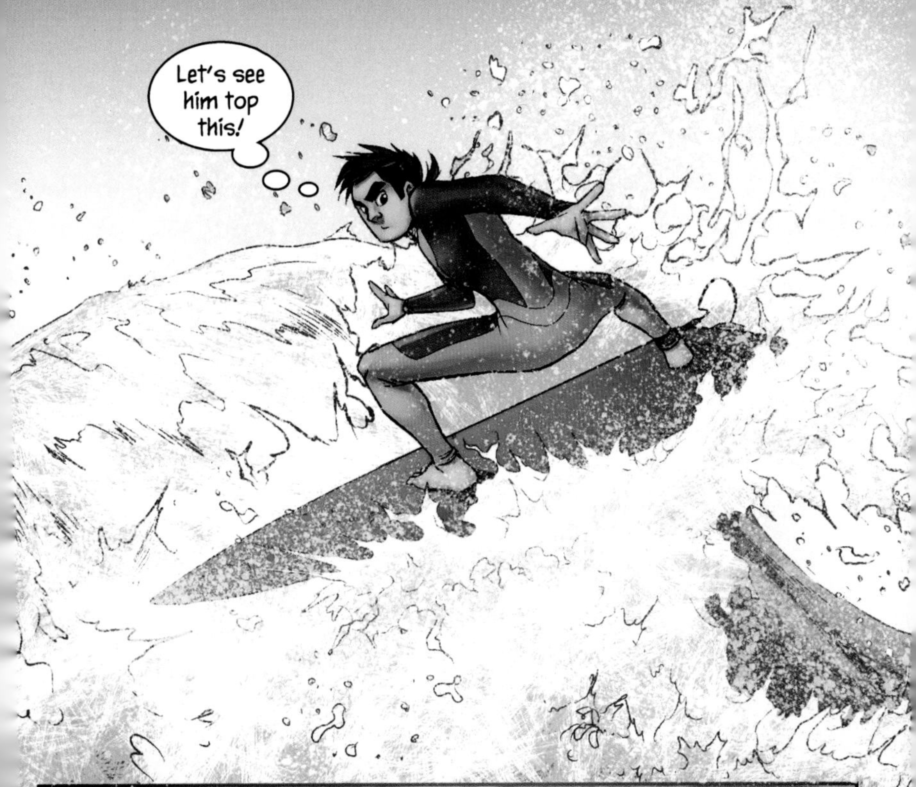
Let's see him top this!

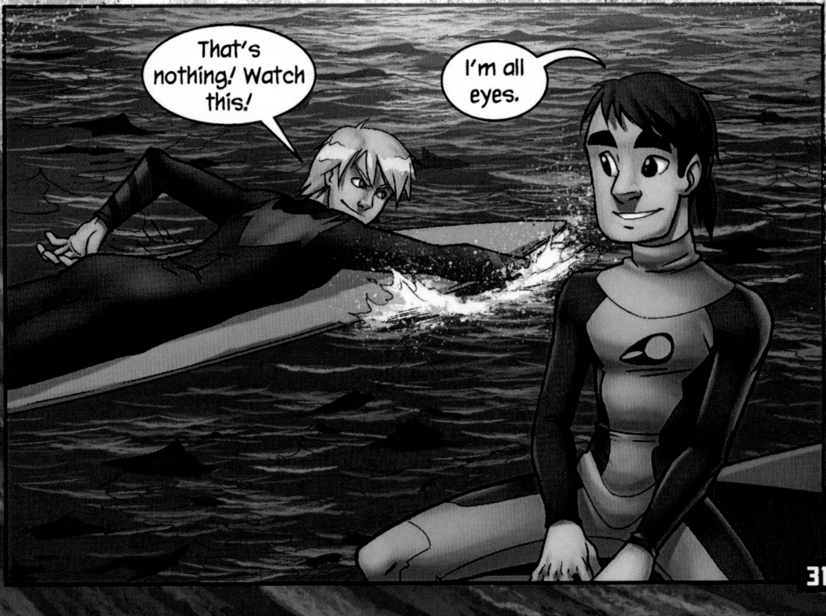
That's nothing! Watch this!
I'm all eyes.

Nailed it!
WHRRRSSH!!
Wow! That was so cool . . .
Told ya.
Just by looking at him, I can tell Cody knows who won.

I head toward Cody. All I can think about are the dangers of Breaker Bay.

The jagged rocks, the strong undertow . . .

Then I see the barrel in front of me. I know I have to take it.

WOOSH!

It's dangerous, but it's also the fastest way to get to Cody.

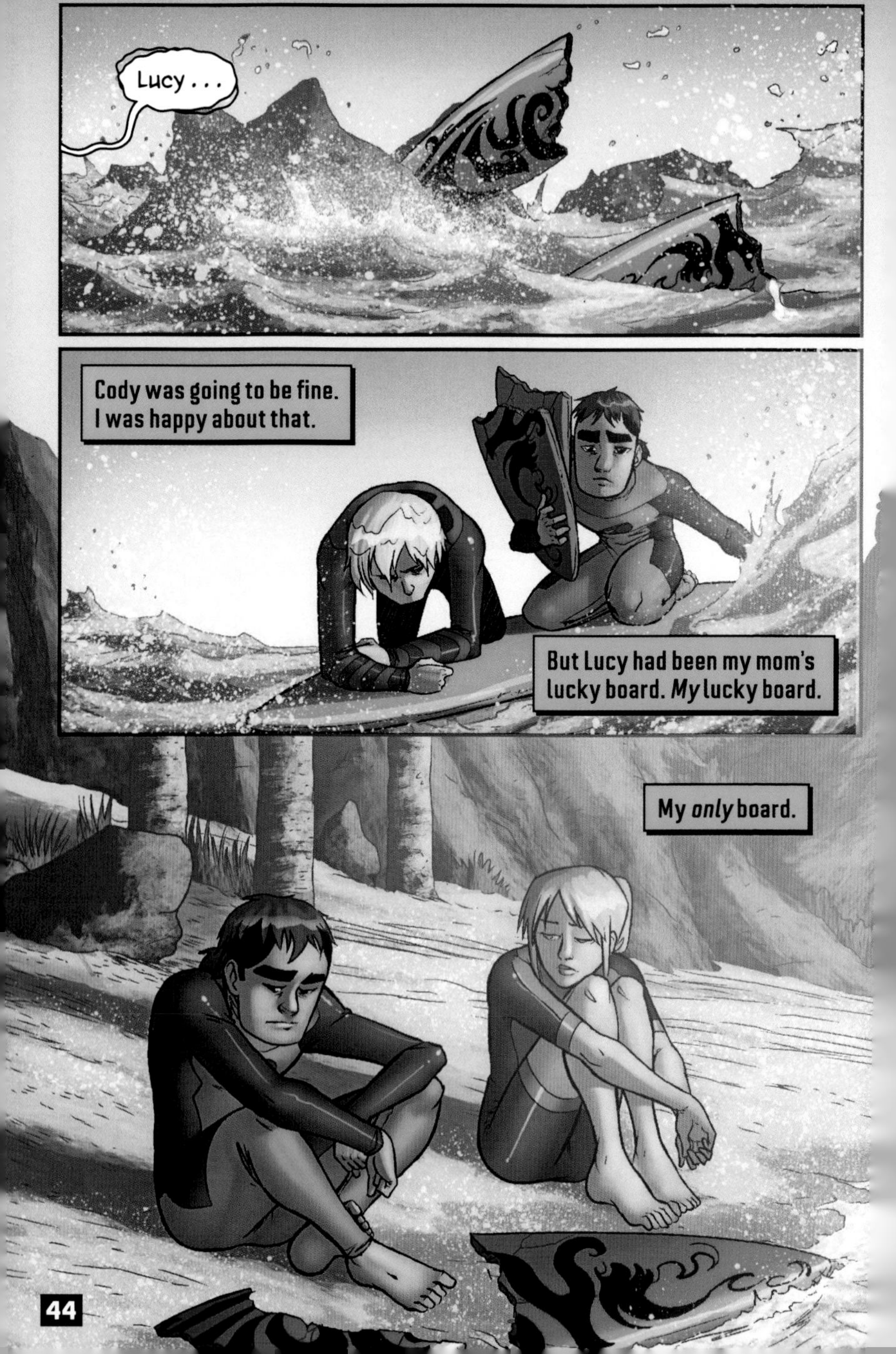
Lucy . . .
Cody was going to be fine.
I was happy about that.
But Lucy had been my mom's
lucky board. *My* lucky board.
My *only* board.

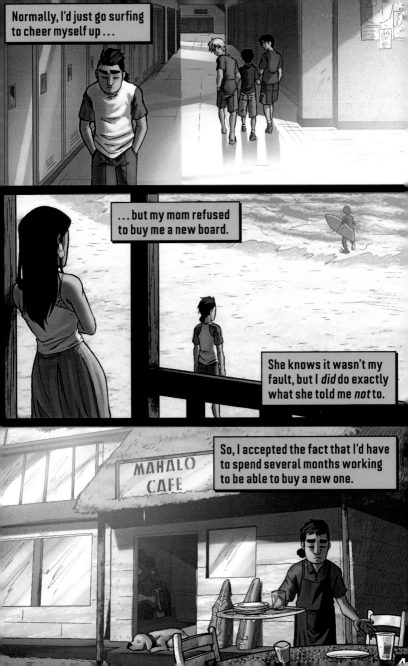

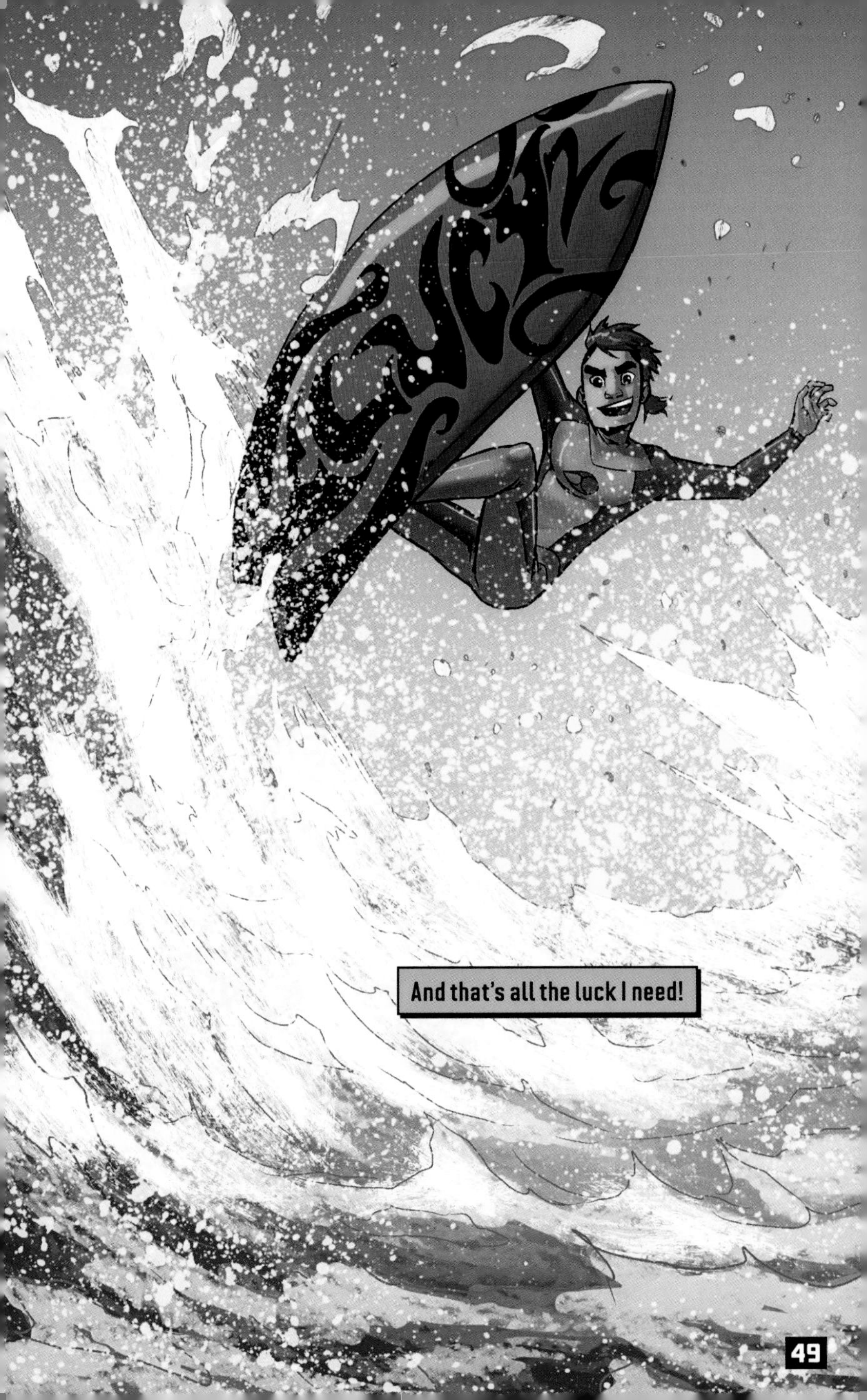
And that's all the luck I need!

BROKEN SURFBOARD LEADS TO NEW FRIENDSHIP

STORY: Cody's ill-advised attempt to surf the wild waves of Breaker Bay led to the destruction of Tane's surfboard, Lucy. However, Tane says that his new board more than makes up for Cody's big mistake. "It was kind of a good thing it happened, actually," Tane says. "For one thing, I realized it wasn't just luck that made me good. And for another, I made a new friend in the process!"

SZ POSTGAME *EXTRA*

WHERE **YOU** ANALYZE THE GAME!

BLZ vs BRS
3-1
RIR vs RDR
33-32
EAG vs BAN
14-7
SPA vs WLD
4-3
BAN vs RDR
21-15
RDR vs LIG
4-3
BRZ vs BRS
3-1

Surfing fans got a real treat today when Tane Kalana one-upped his surfing bully and made a new friend in the process. Let's go into the stands and ask some fans for their opinions on the day's exciting conclusion ...

DISCUSSION QUESTION 1

What are some other ways Tane could have gotten Cody to stop bullying him? Talk about some ways that kids can stop bullies without fighting.

DISCUSSION QUESTION 2

Cody and Tane surf at Breaker Bay despite being told not to. What kinds of things have you done that got you in trouble? Talk about it.

WRITING PROMPT 1

Imagine that you were given your own custom-made surfboard. Write a basic description of the board, then draw a picture of it.

WRITING PROMPT 2

Is Tane a hero for saving Cody like he did? What is your definition of a hero? Have you ever done anything you thought was heroic? Write about it.

(BAYL)—jump off a moving object

(BA-ruhl)—the inside part of a wave that is hollow. It is also known as a "tube."

(FATE)—what will happen to you

(MOK-ing)—making fun of someone

(NUR-vuhss)—easily upset or tense

(ROUND-houss)—a surfing trick that involves a full or half rotation

(soo-pur-STI-shuhss)—if you are superstitious, you believe that good and bad luck can affect you

(TEMPT-ing)—to appeal strongly to, or attract

CREATORS

Brandon Terrell › Author

Brandon Terrell is a writer and filmmaker who has worked in the Minnesota film and television community for nearly ten years. He is the author of the graphic novel *Horrorwood*, published by Ape Entertainment. He is also an avid baseball fan, and is crazy about the Minnesota Twins. Terrell lives in Saint Paul with his wife, Jennifer.

Andres Esparza › Inker

Andres Esparza has been a graphic designer, colorist, and illustrator for many different companies and agencies. Andres now works as a full-time artist for Graphikslava studio in Monterrey, Mexico. In his spare time, Andres loves to play basketball, hang out with family and friends, and listen to good music.

Fernando Cano › Penciler & Colorist

Fernando Cano is an emerging illustrator born in Mexico City, Mexico. He currently resides in Monterrey, Mexico, where he works as a full-time illustrator and colorist at Graphikslava studio. He has done illustration work for Marvel, DC Comics, and role-playing games like Pathfinder from Paizo Publishing. In his spare time, he enjoys hanging out with friends, singing, rowing, and drawing!

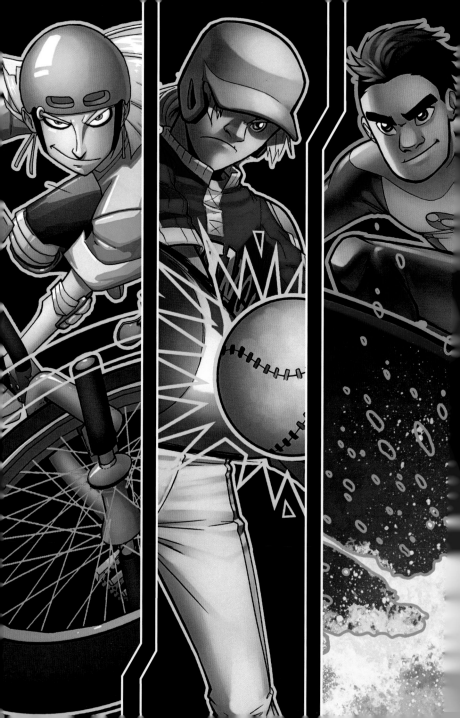

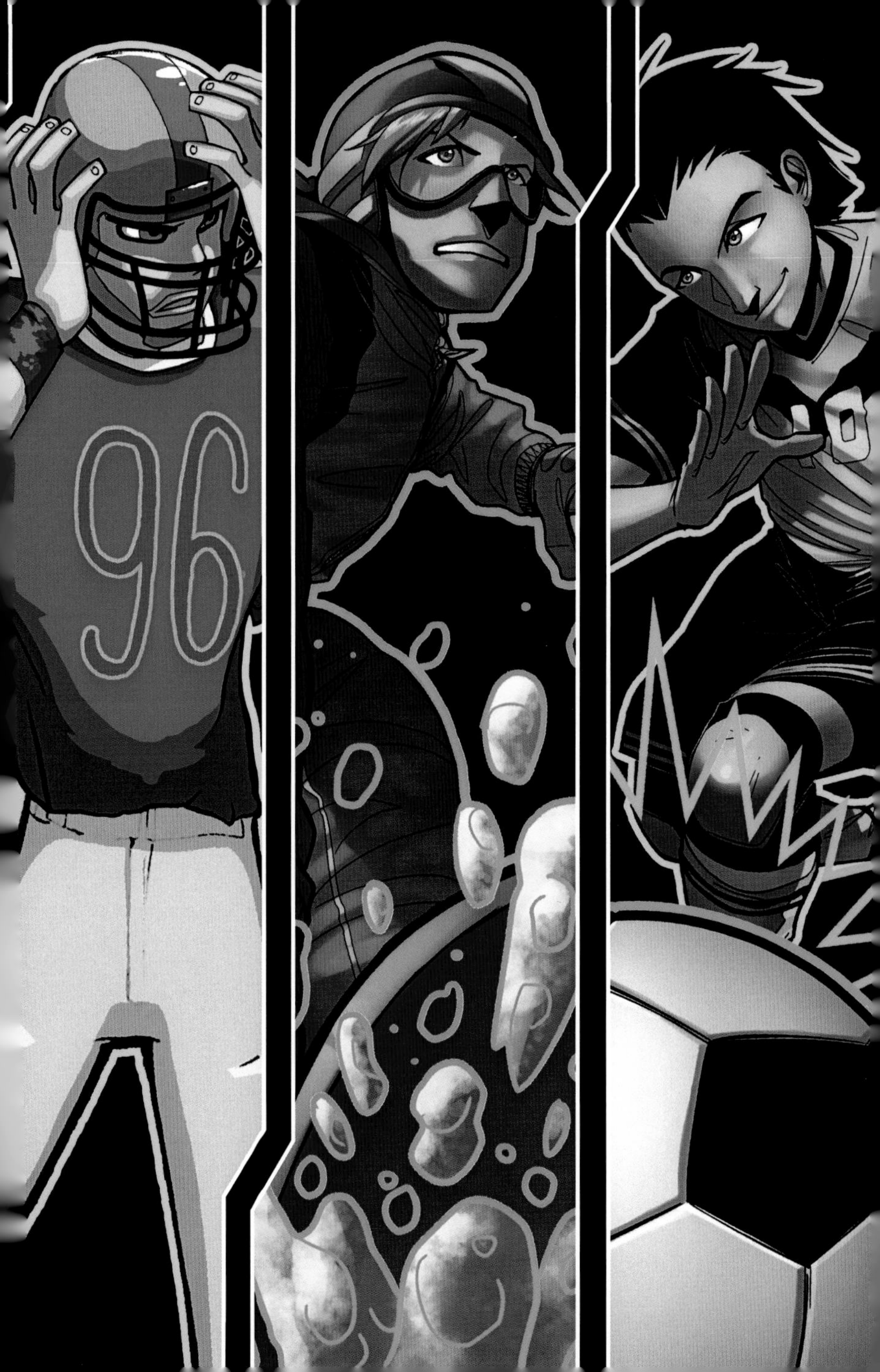
96

Sports Illustrated KIDS

GRAPHIC NOVELS

STONE ARCH BOOKS
a capstone imprint